Gingerbread & Left for Dead

A Short Holiday Mystery

The Laughing Loaf Bakery Mysteries

By Victoria Kazarian

*To my intrepid friends who live, or who have lived,
in the Santa Cruz Mountains*

Story timeframe

Gingerbread & Left for Dead takes place shortly after the events of Laughing Loaf Bakery #4, *Sourdough and Cyanide.*

There is a mild spoiler for *Bread to Rights* (Laughing Loaf #2).

Chapter One

When I stepped out the back door of my bakery that Christmas Eve morning, I shivered at the unexpected chill in the air.

Dark storm clouds had moved in overnight. A heavy moistness hung in the air, as if the sky was lurking just above us, waiting to unload.

Inside, The Laughing Loaf was cheerfully fighting the weather's oppressive vibe. Fresh fir garlands lined the counter, a glittery covering of "snow" dusted countertops, and strings of flashing Christmas lights circled our front windows.

Add to that, a delicious smell pervaded the bakery, coming from the gingerbread cake I was baking and the Christmas spice lattes my assistant Beck Rodriguez was making at the espresso machine.

Maybe the Laughing Loaf Joke of the Day I'd just set out was a little too on the nose.

By Victoria Kazarian

Laughing Loaf Joke of the Day
A gingerbread man went to the doctor,
complaining about his sore knee.
The doctor asked him: "Have you tried icing it?"

The atmosphere in the bakery that day was congenial. Families came in, their kids giddy for the holiday. I'd made a pan of mini cinnamon rolls, and I handed them out for free to the kids who came in. We served up apple cider and spiced lattes as seasonal treats. By the end of the morning, the entire bakery smelled like cinnamon and nutmeg. The smell would cling to me for the next week.

We would close at 1 p.m. today. Beck had a big family celebration to prepare for—all *five* of her brothers, three of them with spouses and young children, were heading up to her parents' house for an overnight sleepover and Christmas celebration. Beck was preparing several dishes and a collection of pastries for their Christmas breakfast and dinner. Christmas was Beck's happy place, and today she was in overdrive, greeting every single customer personally, chatting people up, laughing, and ensuring that everyone left the bakery with a smile on their face.

"Gracie!" Beck called to me from the espresso machine when the crowd had died down. "I have something for you." With Beck and her creative streak, this could mean she painted me a picture, invented a new pastry, or made a whimsical sign to advertise our latest baked offering.

"Okay, close your eyes, Gracie. And smell this." She held something up to my nose, something warm and fragrant, scented with nutmeg.

"Keep your eyes closed." I heard excitement bubbling over in Beck's voice. "Now tell me what you think it is."

Memories filtered through my head of Christmases

past. "It can't be—is it an eggnog latte?" I could hear Beck suppressing laughter.

"You can open your eyes now."

She handed me a mug topped with whipped cream. "You told me once how much you loved them. You always say you can't find them anywhere. I bought my own eggnog so I could make it here. Merry Christmas."

If the moody weather outside was bringing me down, this gave me a big dose of Christmas cheer. I took a sip of the creamy, fragrant latte.

I reached around her, hot latte in one hand, and gave her a side hug, tears in my eyes. "This is the best present I could ask for this morning."

Eggnog lattes had been my late mom's and my holiday tradition when I was a preteen. We'd get them in Seattle after Christmas shopping. Unfortunately, Starbucks and most other places stopped making them. Beck's treat filled me with nostalgia and renewed excitement for the holiday.

Even though the dark clouds gathering outside were scaring me—just a little.

Longtime River Grove residents had told me war stories of torrential rains and downed trees blocking roads; power outages that lasted days. Before that first winter, I kept wood stocked for our wood-fired stove at home. If the power went out, at least we'd be warm. And, hey, maybe we could roast marshmallows.

Since moving to the small town of River Grove, I often asked myself: why do people choose to live here?

Life wasn't easy in the mountains. But the rough life gave River Grovians a sense of pride. If you lived here for five years or so, you learned how to handle almost anything. River Grovians carried chainsaws and work boots in their vehicles. It was best to be prepared, since you didn't know how fast the county or state would be able to fix things. A few years ago, when a downed tree blocked Highway 17, mountain dwellers didn't wait for road crews to show up. They pulled out their chainsaws and cleared the tree themselves, organizing stranded drivers to pass the tree chunks to the side of the road.

River Grove was nestled in the Santa Cruz Mountains, a beautiful place with sloping wooded hills, a glimpse of the ocean six miles away, and acres of massive hundred-year-old redwood trees. Downtown River Grove had a laid-back, old-timey feel, and it only got busy in the summer, when everyone wanted to cut through the mountains to get to the beaches off Highway 1.

Just twenty-five miles to the east, cars sped along busy freeways heading for the business parks of Silicon Valley—a completely different world.

If you wanted to hide out from civilization for a while, River Grove was the place. You could be part of a tight-knit community of people who had your back.

Or, you could hole up in your cabin and live off the grid.

By that Christmas, I'd lived in River Grove for almost two years. After testifying against my husband, who'd been selling defense secrets to foreign governments, federal witness protection relocated me, my dog, and my father, Dr. John Markley, to River Grove. My father chose to retire from teaching physics at the university so he could be with me, his only child.

I'd had my fill of the tech industry, where I'd worked with my husband in Seattle. I went back to something I'd loved growing up—baking bread. After my mother passed away when I was fifteen, baking bread had become my happy place.

With the help of the $60,000 I received as part of my

relocation package from WITSEC, I started The Laughing Loaf Bakery in an old brick bank building on the main highway through River Grove.

Hiring Beck as my assistant quickly became the best decision I'd ever made. We built The Laughing Loaf into a community gathering place, serving really good coffee, an assortment of breads, and a tasty menu of pastries that made our bakery one of the best spots in the mountains to get a bite to eat.

Even though the circumstances that brought me to River Grove were pretty traumatic, I was surprised to find that my life had undergone a major upgrade. I learned a valuable lesson—you can't always tell a good break from a bad one. Something that seems like a horrible turn of fate can become the thing that changes your life for the better.

TONIGHT, for Christmas Eve, Reggie McFerrin, proprietor of the popular music venue The Riverside Saloon, was hosting a concert and Christmas Eve buffet for River Grovians.

Dave Westerman, River Grove chief of police, had come into the bakery that morning with Mayor Corinne Webster to have their usual morning coffee and to talk about public safety at the corner table in the dining room.

The chief unbuttoned his heavy jacket as he waited at the counter for his coffee. "It might look scary out there right now, but don't worry, Gracie. The big storms don't come till January at the earliest. If we're lucky, we'll get a little snow on the peaks in time for Christmas. Never lasts, though."

"You going to The Riverside tonight?" I asked the chief.

"Yes, but I have to drive out to do a welfare check before

that. Some woman in Half Moon Bay can't reach her father and she's worried about him with the storm coming in." He brightened up. "But I'm sure looking forward to the buffet tonight. Chloe and her mother are coming with me. April Lewis, Noah Thornton Bell's kid, is playing violin with the band. So of course, Corinne's going to be there."

I waved at the stern Corinne Webster—aka Mayor C to our town and "Auntie Corrie" to April, her godchild. She looked up from whatever she was poring over at the table, gave me a curt nod and a frown, then went back to her reading.

My boyfriend Nate, and my father and his girlfriend Mary Jo, were attending tonight. Nate would ride over on his bike—hopefully before the rain hit us—and we'd drive down to The Riverside together at 6:30.

"We'll see you there, Chief," I said as I passed him his drip coffee. He made his way to the corner table to sit down with Mayor C, his partner in preventing crime.

At noon, my best friend Elana came up to the counter, carrying a sparkly bag filled with tissue paper—which along with pink pastry boxes, is something that always gets my attention.

"Gracie, I know you're busy." She smiled and handed me the bag. "I brought a little something for you and for Biga."

I shook the bag excitedly and tried to peek in through the tissue. "Thanks, my friend. You going to The Riverside tonight?"

"I want to. Kirk's wiped out from a hard week at Blue-Soft." Elana sighed as she leaned against the counter. "We did Hannukah with his family and had get-togethers all last week. Christmas is my holiday to celebrate, but now that it's here, Kirk's run out of steam."

"Then why don't you come with us? It's going to be fun. It's Nate, my dad, Mary Jo, and I. Reggie's serving a big buffet and there'll be music till midnight." I saw her eyes light up. Elana was, in ways ABBA would approve, the quintessential dancing queen.

"Sure! If it's ok to crash the party."

"You're not crashing at all. Reggie'd love to have you there. Meet us there at 6:30."

Elana reached over the counter to give me a hug, a look of gratitude in her eyes. "I didn't want to stay home."

"I know." I grinned at her. "See you there."

It took forever to get to 1 p.m. I locked the front door and hung up the CLOSED sign with the picture of the snoozing bread loaf on it. I turned on Christmas music in the back room. Beck and I wiped down tables and counters, while singing along loudly, of course.

Biga let out a howl, but he wasn't singing along with us —he was reminding me that he was still there, just in case I forgot.

The boy needed his time outside.

Biga had been in his pen in the side room for a while. When he saw me enter with his leash, he started spinning in circles, almost falling over himself with joy.

I shivered as we walked down the back steps to the alley. I had to check my phone to make sure it was 1:15, not 5:15 p.m.

The sky had darkened. Clouds overhead felt low and heavy, as fog wound through the redwoods, tightening its grip on the treetops. We walked down the alley and onto the trail that followed the river. As soon as we merged onto the treelined trail, the light dimmed, and the air temperature seemed to dip by 20 degrees.

I held onto the chief's words: it was too early in the

season for a major storm. Still, it was hard to keep my holiday mood up with clouds like this bearing down on us. I remembered stories I'd heard from River Grove old timers, about downed trees, washed-out roads, and houses sliding down hillsides.

After Biga had a chance to do his thing on nearly every bush and weed along the path, we turned around and headed back to the bakery.

Sharp, cold drops of rain started pelting me as we made our way to the back door.

Since we didn't have to prep for tomorrow's bakes—we'd be closed for two days—our remaining chores would be quick this afternoon. Beck cleaned the front counter and espresso machine while I washed utensils in the back room and fed the tub of sourdough starter.

I wouldn't see Beck for two days, which seemed incredibly long, since I usually saw my cheery, hardworking co-worker every day.

"Have a wonderful Christmas with the family, Beck." I handed her a gift bag, containing a set of copper molds for making the custardy French pastries called *canelés*. I'd found the molds on a recent trip to San Francisco. I knew she'd been wanting them.

"Thank you, Gracie!" Beck peeked inside then held the package to her chest. "How did you know I've been trying to make these at home? I can't wait to use these."

She hugged me. After locking up, we made a run for our cars. I clutched Biga's crate as I dodged steady raindrops.

By the time I pulled into our carport at home, drops were pummeling the carport roof so rapidly it sounded like a dump truck was unloading gravel onto it. I took Biga's crate out and hurried into the house.

My father let us in, then stood in the doorway staring out at the onslaught of rain.

"I haven't seen rain like this since we left Seattle." He shut the door. "And I think this might be worse."

"The chief swears this won't be the big one. River Grove doesn't see major storms till at least January," I said, releasing Biga from his crate. "Since he's been here longer than we have, he's probably right. But this is intense."

I needed something to warm me up before I started wrapping gifts for tonight.

"Hot chocolate, dad?"

"Just tea for me, dear." My father called distractedly on his way to his study, shuffling down the hall in his slippers.

I felt like calling down the hall: "You know, it's very easy to *make it yourself*." But I was feeling generous today, excited about tonight's celebration.

After flipping on the electric kettle for tea, I made my hot chocolate on the stove in a small saucepan. I added whole milk, sugar, vanilla, and a dash of salt. When it got hot, I added cocoa powder and a shake of cinnamon and whisked it all together.

I poured it, steaming, into a big stoneware mug. Wrapping my hands around it warmed me up.

I wished my boyfriend Nate could be here to share a cup with me while cuddling on the couch. He was in his photography shed today, developing photos from a wildlife shoot he'd done in Yosemite a few weeks ago.

I let my dad's tea steep for the precise four minutes that he wanted, then added milk, and put it on a tray with a shortbread wafer to take back to him.

Then I pulled my treasure stash out of my closet and sat down on the couch to begin wrapping. I delighted in finding just the right gifts for my loved ones, but I wasn't a fan of wrapping.

So, I'd bought a huge stack of gift bags and tissue paper. How long does it take to rip open a present? Seconds. I'm not giving up ten minutes of my life to wrap something.

When shopping for people, I use my listening and investigative skills to pick up clues as to what they would like.

I got my dad a book on physicist Nikola Tesla that he'd been admiring online—judging by the many times I'd caught him looking it up on his computer. The hardback book was easily stashed in a bag, but it was *very* heavy.

For Nate, I'd gotten a little more creative. Lately, he'd been saying he was bored with his coffeemaker. A little more questioning revealed that he missed the coffee he'd had during his photography internship in Italy years ago, so I'd gotten him a Bialetti moka pot for making espresso on the little stove in his photo shed. Plus, I had one of my favorite photos of his made into a card. It was a close-up of a finch from his Galapagos Islands trip. The bird was cocking its head, glaring straight at the camera with a look that said, "*Um*, a little privacy here?"

My father's girlfriend Mary Jo often wore hats, and one of The Laughing Loaf's long-time customers made adorable, felted ones. I'd commissioned her to make a dark blue cloche that would look great on Mary Jo.

I wrapped it carefully in tissue and slipped it into a gift bag.

For Elana, I'd found a recording on vinyl of one of her favorite bands, which both of us had seen play at The Riverside. I wrapped it in tissue and slipped it into a bag along with a rhinestone-encrusted band for her high tech watch.

Biga was giving me a look: *Very nice. Where's my present?*

"You thought I forgot you?" I pulled a chew toy out of my goody bag. It was his favorite kind: It had a nice, satisfying squeak and was made of soft yet durable plastic he could sink his teeth into. On top of that, it was *bacon* scented. I made it squeak, then threw it. He galloped away to get it. We did this, oh, maybe ten more times.

Then I remembered the gift bag Elana had given me, which I'd shoved into my tote bag when I left the bakery.

Inside there was a bag of treats for Biga. Elana and Kirk were very familiar with Biga's food obsession.

I also found a package with a silky green top for me, woven through with glowy, iridescent threads. It was totally Elana—not something I'd have picked out for myself. But it was beautiful, and I decided I'd wear it to The Riverside tonight.

A little before 6 p.m., I was dressed and ready—wearing boots, my new shiny top, warm pants, and a waterproof jacket. One glance out my front window, and I saw the downpour was still going strong, and now the wind had whipped up. The streetlight revealed tree branches strewn across the wet street.

I called Nate.

"Don't know if you've looked outside lately. This isn't exactly bicycle weather."

"Uh, I just noticed that." He must be in his photography shed. I heard a barrage of rain pounding down on its light roof. "Damn. My power just went out. But I'm ready if you want to pick me up. Come by anytime."

If Nate's power went out, ours probably would, too. So far, we'd only had one power outage during our time in

River Grove, and it was fixed by the next morning. What would we do if it lasted for days?

Maybe I was worrying too much. The storm would pass through in a day or two. It might end up being an inconvenience, but we'd be fine.

My father came out of his study, dressed in a bright red sweater and khaki slacks, his trench coat in his arms. He clasped his hands together.

"Are we ready, dear? Mary Jo called and asked if we could pick her up on our way. She doesn't feel comfortable driving in the rain."

"No problem," I said, gathering up the bags I'd filled and putting them in a crate. "We better leave soon. Nate needs a ride, too. He can't ride his bike in this weather."

With the storm, I didn't want to leave Biga at home by himself, so I'd texted Reggie to see if there was place for him at The Riverside.

Reggie had a soft spot for my dog. He responded that if I brought a doggie gate, Biga could hang out in the storage room off the kitchen.

Relieved, I went out to the carport with my dad and Biga in his crate. It was only a few feet, but by the time we got to the car, we were drenched.

After loading Biga and his gate in the car, I pressed the ignition and turned on the heat.

"This will be an adventure." My father chuckled as he got into the back seat. "I know you say otherwise, Gracie, but you do love adventures."

I raised my eyebrows at him in the rearview mirror. "As long as I get to choose them myself."

When we pulled up in front of Nate's house, he came out of his front door, a large backpack slung over his shoulder.

"Nate, I saved the front seat for you," my dad called from the back seat. "Your legs wouldn't fit back here."

"Thank you, John." My six-foot-four boyfriend turned and nodded at my dad in the back seat. "Gracie, I just got a text from Sam. He and Beck made it to her parents' house safely. Beck wanted you to know. And they just lost power."

"That'll be a crazy night, with all those kids." I started the car and we headed for the highway.

Mary Jo lived next to Growing Affection, the plant nursery she ran just outside of town. As I pulled out onto the highway, I realized how hard it would be to navigate. Rain was coming down in torrents and lights were out in houses and businesses along the way, which made it hard to mark where we were.

But with my father's directions, I found Mary Jo's house, set back behind the chain-link fence surrounding the nursery. Potted trees in the nursery yard had toppled over onto each other like a row of dominos. The place would need a lot of cleanup.

Mary Jo's porch light was on and there were lights behind the window curtains.

"I've got my umbrella. I'll run up to get her." My father opened his door to get out, only to be hit by a slap of sideways rain that turned his umbrella inside out.

"John, why not let me go?" Nate got out of the car, pulled his jacket hood around his head and forged his way up the walk to Mary Jo's door.

A few minutes later, he escorted my dad's girlfriend down the steps and toward our car. She eased into the back seat next to my dad, and we were on our way to The Riverside.

"Thank you, Gracie." Mary Jo settled into the back seat. As I backed out of the driveway, we watched a long wooden fence in the nursery's yard flop over in the wind, as if pushed by unseen hands.

"Oh dear," she sighed heavily. "This is *not* looking good."

Chapter Two

fter the drive through darkened areas of town, the brightly lit Riverside Saloon was a welcoming sight, its double doors and roofline decorated with white Christmas lights.

I felt the thump of live music before I heard it. The lot was about half full, and we weren't the only ones arriving a little late. Couples and families eased themselves out of their cars, sheltering their heads with rain hats and umbrellas, probably as thankful as we were to have survived the drive. Rain continued to pelt us all as we made our way to the door. Biga, huddled in his warm, dry crate, had it easy compared to the rest of us. He was probably sleeping through this.

Once inside, we gazed in awe at the lavishly decorated main floor of The Riverside. With its high ceiling and rustic wood paneling, it looked like a mountain lodge, and the air smelled woodsy and fresh. Natural fir garlands festooned with lights and red ribbons lined the room. Between the bar and the massive stone fireplace, an enormous Christmas tree extended nearly to the top of the high ceiling, decorated with a bright gold star, white lights, and shimmering globes in indigo—Reggie's favorite color.

Over on the stage, a band played instrumental Christmas music. April Lewis, still sporting bright pink hair, was dressed in a sedate, long black dress. She played violin along with a keyboard player, bass player, and electric guitarist—on a lively jazz variation of "God Rest Ye Merry Gentlemen."

Guests were helping themselves at a long buffet table lined with fir garlands which featured meats, vegetable dishes, salads, finger food, and a row of sumptuous Christmas desserts. I was thrilled to see Reggie's homemade guacamole set up next to the finger foods, by a bowl of tortilla chips. I could practically see my name written all over that section of the buffet.

Nate turned to me, his eyebrows raised. "I don't know that I've ever seen anything like this."

"Reggie loves to treat his friends." I leaned into Nate, feeling happy to be in this place with him tonight. It might have been an ordeal getting here, but it was worth it.

I set down Biga's crate and his gate, as I looked around for Reggie.

"We're going to go find us a table," Mary Jo said purposefully as she linked arms with my father. They walked past the buffet to the tables, as I scanned the room to see if Elana was here yet.

I turned around when I heard a familiar voice.

"Gracie!" Elana said excitedly as she and Kirk approached.

"You both came!" I hugged each one of them.

"Thanks for the beautiful top," I whispered to Elana, opening my coat to show her.

"I knew it! That's *totally* your color, girl," she said with a smile.

"I couldn't let Elana go out by herself on a night like this," Kirk said, a sheepish look on his face. "I also remembered Reggie throws a damn good party."

"Good to see you, Kirk." Nate greeted him with a man hug and pat on the back.

"Why don't you all go find your seats at the table?" I said, waving to my dad and Mary Jo at the far end of the room. They'd snagged a nice long table—next to one with Chief Westerman, Renee, and Chloe.

While they began chatting, I picked up Biga's crate and went looking for our host.

Drake, the bartender, told me Reggie had gone upstairs to his office.

I made my way up the back stairs, flashbacks playing in my head of the night Reggie had smuggled Elana and me upstairs when Russian spies tried to track me down for my ex-husband's tech secrets. Reggie had gotten us out of a dangerous situation. He'd probably saved our lives.

Reggie sat in his purple leather office chair, looking out his large picture window at the blur of dark clouds, deep in thought.

As usual, he was dressed in a black suit, a stark contrast to his pale skin—which made me think of a hippie vampire when I'd first met him. His almost unnaturally black hair was pulled back in a low ponytail, his eyes invisible behind shaded glasses. His one concession to the holiday was a red bow tie.

When he stood up, I saw the tense, brooding look on his face. "I'm sorry. I should have been down there to meet you and Biga."

Biga whimpered in his crate. He recognized Reggie's

voice. I opened the crate and my little dog tumbled out, heading to his favorite person.

Reggie picked him up and nuzzled him.

"Is everything okay, Reggie?"

He gave me a tired smile.

"I have news to share, but I'll do it after dinner. It's Christmas. After all, I invited everyone here to celebrate."

Reggie still held Biga as we walked downstairs, to a room off the kitchen used for storing table linens, room partitions, and extra chairs. I set up Biga's special blanket, a chew stick, and a few of his toys, then Reggie set Biga down.

"We'll check in on you soon, Biga," Reggie said as we stepped outside, and I locked the gate in place. I'd saved one final toy, one of his favorites. I threw it and when Biga immediately scampered after it, we made our escape.

"Thanks, Reggie. I didn't feel comfortable leaving him at home."

"Wise decision, Gracie." Reggie looked at me soberly. His phone buzzed. He pulled it out and checked something, then frowned.

Puzzled and a little worried about what Reggie would announce, I went back to our table.

I passed by the buffet, but the sumptuous foods—and even the guac and chips—no longer seemed as appealing. But since this was Reggie's guacamole, I filled a bowl with the guac and some chips, then went to take my seat next to Nate. Across the table, Mary Jo was gesturing excitedly, talking to Elana about some restaurant she'd just visited in Santa Cruz. My father had pushed his plate of meat and vegetables aside. He was digging into what looked like a piece of authentic English mince pie. He had no compunction about eating dessert first.

Nate leaned in toward me. "Everything okay?"

"Biga's settled in a room near the kitchen," I said, trying to look calm. "He should be fine."

He shot me a curious look. "I wasn't asking about Biga. You looked upset when you came downstairs."

I whispered back. "Reggie's upset about something. I've never seen him like this."

"The storm?" Nate sawed off a piece of his prime rib.

"I think so." I dipped a chip into the guac. "Which makes me more scared."

A half an hour later, as people sat at their tables finishing dessert, Reggie got up on stage and took the microphone.

For a moment, the lights above us flickered, as if they were going off. Then they came back on again, and Reggie's voice came through the loudspeaker.

"I just got a call from a friend at county emergency services. At first, this storm was forecast to blow through by Christmas Day. Now they're saying it's an atmospheric river. It's going to sit over the Bay Area and Santa Cruz Mountains for three days at the least, a week at the most."

A man called out from one of the back tables.

"Reggie, what does that mean? Is this going to be worse than the storm a two years ago?"

Reggie was approaching eighty, though he usually didn't look it. Today, worry had etched lines into his face.

"The river will flood, which will affect anyone living close to it. Roads will probably wash out, like the sinkhole we had up on Highway 35 a few years ago. Trees will go down. We'll have landslides. Then there's the power outages. PG&E won't be able to restore service for days. They'll be swamped."

Reggie paused and took a drink. I wasn't sure if it was water or something stronger. He took a deep breath.

By Victoria Kazarian

"Most of you here have seen rough weather in River Grove. In recent years, things have gotten more intense. This storm will be up there with the worst we've seen. Please consider your surroundings and stay safe. If you think you can ride this out at home—if you're by the river, or a vulnerable hillside—think again.

"If your property is in danger tonight, move to higher ground. Think about staying with friends—and you are always welcome to stay here at The Riverside. We have room for you here. Our generator will kick in when the power goes out. There's no reason for anyone to leave."

My heart sunk. Apparently, my dad and I had gotten off easy in our past two years in River Grove. We'd had days of rain, and we'd seen the river rise, but nothing like what Reggie was describing. I worried about Beck and her family, celebrating together without power, in the hills off of a one-lane road that had washed out many times.

"What can we do?" Someone called out from a table near us.

"Stick together, help each other out. We need to keep an eye out for our neighbors." Reggie's face tightened. "I'm sorry if this scares you, my friends. Life in River Grove is not for the fainthearted. But most of you have figured that out by now."

It scared me. Easygoing Reggie never talked like this, had never looked this worried.

The roomful of people sat looking at Reggie. Then they turned to each other in a daze.

Flooding would hit those of us near the river first.

If the storm would be as bad as Reggie had told us, none of us could guarantee our houses, workplaces, and property would be there tomorrow morning.

Chapter Three

Conversation at the tables rose to a rumble. Some people got up and left, heading to check on their houses and property. A few went up to Reggie, maybe asking about staying the night.

I dipped a chip in guacamole and started eating, thinking about what Reggie had told us. Our backyard was about fifty yards from the river, but Nate's photography shed was fifteen feet from the shore.

"Your photo gallery and your equipment—how easily can those be moved from the shed?" I asked.

Nate looked at me with concern. He rubbed his face. "I need to get them out tonight. I can see if Brad Castro can help with the equipment—" Nate turned around to see if he could spot the police deputy in the room.

"How about Kirk?" I asked. Then I realized both Elana and Kirk, sitting on the other side of my dad and Mary Jo, were watching us.

"What's going on?" Kirk looked over at us with a smile. "I just heard my name."

As Nate told him how close his shed was to the river,

Kirk frowned. "Of course. Let's get everything out tonight. We should be able to fit everything in my SUV. You can keep it at our place as long as you need to."

I heard negotiations going on at the tables around us:

"There's no way this is as bad as Reggie says. We'll ride this one out. We've done it before."

"Can we stay with your sister in San Jose?"

"I'll get the dogs in the car, and we'll drive down to Watsonville before it gets bad."

Behind us at the next table, the chief was preparing to leave with his daughter and granddaughter.

"Chief, you're not going to sit this one out at home, are you?" I asked.

His daughter Renee turned to me and lowered her voice. "I'm giving him no choice. We're staying here. We've had bad luck in previous storms—trees down all over our property, power out for two weeks."

"We'd be fine at home, Renee. They're making a big deal out of this," the chief said with a grunt. "I've lived here for over ten years, and we've always gotten through it."

"Chief, doesn't it make sense for you to stay closer to City Hall?" I asked. "If there's an emergency, it'll be easier to respond."

Renee nodded. "She's right, Dad. Let's ask Reggie about a room."

I heard Mary Jo and my dad talking in serious tones.

Eventually, Mary Jo and my father decided to take Reggie up on his offer and stay at The Riverside for the night. I turned to Nate, who'd been planning the logistics of the trip to the shed with Kirk.

I turned to him and whispered. "When you're done, how would you feel about staying here for the night?"

Nate's lips turned up into his classic not-trying-to-smile

smile. He slipped his hand into mine, under the table. "Kirk and Elana offered to put us up at their place, but I thought you'd want to be near the bakery to keep an eye on it. Let's stay here."

The music hall was emptying out, as River Grovians made their decisions. Reggie's staff offered people insulated takeout bags for storing food from the buffet, since most people here had lost power and wouldn't be able to cook. There was no lingering to talk. Mary Jo and my dad went up to talk to Reggie about staying. I followed them.

Violin case in one hand, April Lewis was getting ready to leave with Mayor C.

"April, I loved hearing you play tonight." I gave the young musician a hug. "I wish we could talk. How long are you in town?"

She shrugged. "I don't have another gig till New Year's Eve. I had dinner with my grandfather last night, and I want to see him again. I like the idea of staying in one place." Her eyes lit up. "And this storm is kind of... *exciting.*" Words from someone who didn't own a home and could easily pick up and leave after the storm ended.

I hugged Mayor C, who seemed stressed. For the next week, her town would be under siege.

"You okay, Gracie?" She asked, concern in her voice. "You're close to the river. Three years ago, a redwood came down on your property. Smashed the couple's gazebo to bits and narrowly missed the house. Just something to watch for."

This was something the realtor hadn't told us. I grimaced. *Thanks for the comforting news, mayor.*

"We'll check the house tomorrow. I'm staying here tonight," I told the mayor. "Kirk and Nate are driving over to get the equipment out of his photo shed."

Just when I'd started to feel comforted at the thought of staying the night in a nice cozy room at The Riverside, fear surged through me. What if a tree *did* fall on our house? What if Nate's photography shed washed away? The Laughing Loaf was downtown, in a safer area, but still— storm damage and flooding could keep us closed for weeks.

I went in and checked on Biga, asleep on his blanket, oblivious to everything going on. Chew toys and nuggets of food were strewn across the floor. He lifted his head. When he saw me, he popped up, his tail wagging. I sat down cross-legged on the floor, and he curled up on my lap, rubbing his head against my leg. He was shaking, in that way chihuahuas do when they're happy, excited, scared, or just overwhelmed.

I sat with him for a while, cuddling him but also getting my bearings as I thought about Reggie's news.

"Let's go outside so you can do your thing." I opened the gate, and we headed for the back door, which opened out onto a patio and small yard overlooking the river, about twenty feet down and fifty yards away. It wouldn't reach us at The Riverside, but even at this point, the current below was strong, surging over rocks now submerged.

Biga hated getting wet. He gave me a wide-eyed, forlorn look, then gingerly padded around the wet patio until he found a bush at the edge of the yard. When he was finished, he tugged on the leash for us to go back inside.

Nate met me as we came in the door. His lips brushed my cheek.

"Kirk and I are heading out now in the SUV. He'll drop me off when we're done. Shouldn't take us more than forty minutes. Oh, and Reggie says no problem bringing Biga up to the room."

"Thanks for asking." I leaned against his chest and sighed with relief. "Now please be careful."

Reggie had taken my dad and Mary Jo upstairs, so I held Biga as I looked out the front windows. The last of the invitees were ducking down, sheltering with umbrellas as they got into their cars. A growing puddle in the middle of the parking lot reflected back a strange, distorted version of The Riverside's festive lights.

The large, high-ceilinged hall around me was still decorated for the holiday, but the garlands and lights were a sad reminder that this was supposed to be a celebration. The staff was clearing off tables and stacking plates. Others removed chafing pans from the buffet, loaded them on carts and trundled them back to the kitchen.

"Gracie." Reggie called to me from near the front doors, as he said goodbye to another group of guests. "I've got your key. Your father and Mary Jo are across the hall."

"Thank you so much, Reggie."

Carrying Biga, I took the key and went up the staircase to our room, my legs tired from a long stressful day.

I opened the door, closed it behind me, and looked at the four-poster bed, covered with a patchwork quilt made of purple and indigo patterned fabrics. I realized this was the room I'd stayed in last summer when I was helping April Lewis, after her musician father Noah Thornton Bell had just been killed. An antique upright piano stood against the far wall.

I sat down and played a verse of "Silent Night," my hands moving across the keys instinctively. Playing the familiar song felt comforting and reminded me of my mother, who'd played it every Christmas morning to signal us it was time to get up and unwrap presents. Then I smiled as I played Mozart's "Rondo alla Turca," which made me sound like a way better piano player than I really was.

I stretched out on the large bed. I only realized after I'd laid down that the bed was way too high for Biga to jump up on.

Biga looked up at me pitifully, trying to figure out whether he could jump up. I held out my arms and hauled him up onto the bed next to me. He curled up by my legs, ready to settle in for the night.

At 9:15, I looked out the window to see eerie darkness where downtown River Grove should be. Raindrops hit the window like tiny bullets.

Nate should be back in about a half an hour, assuming the roads were clear, and that he and Kirk could fit the computer, storage files, and darkroom equipment in the SUV.

Since I'd gotten up at 4 a.m. for bakery prep, I was exhausted. I dozed off, lulled by the rhythm of the rain on the roof.

A deep roll of thunder jarred me awake. Down by my leg, Biga growled.

I sat up immediately. I reached for my phone and checked for a text from Nate.

Nothing from him. It was 10:20 p.m.

I got off the bed, slipped my phone into my pocket and picked Biga up.

I padded downstairs in my socks, realizing I was still wearing what I'd worn to dinner. The stiff fabric in the shiny top Elana had given me made my neck itch. I'd give anything for a t-shirt right now.

Downstairs, The Riverside staff was setting out fruit, cereal, and granola bars on the tables, for guests wanting a snack.

I didn't see any other guests. Or Nate.

I sat down with Biga on my lap and texted him.

You ok?

Still with Kirk?

I waited a few minutes. I wanted a response--anything. My stomach knotted up.

I'd call Elana to see if she'd heard anything from Kirk. Hopefully she'd charged her phone, and her power and network connections were holding up.

She picked up on the first ring.

"Have you heard anything from Kirk? The guys were supposed to be back an hour ago."

"No, and I'm getting nervous," Elana said. "It's really bad out there."

I took a seat at one of the tables near the front windows. "If Nate's not back in a half an hour, I'm going to go find the chief. He's staying here. I'll let you know if I find out anything."

I reached over and grabbed a granola bar. Reggie's guac and chips, as good as they were, had not been a meal.

I'd just taken a bite when The Riverside's front doors flew open, letting in a blast of wind and rain, along with Nate, Kirk, and the chief, all of them drenched.

My stomach dropped. I stood up.

Nate's hair was saturated, and his eyes looked haunted.

"Gracie, when we were loading up the equipment I found a body in the river."

Chapter Four

Reggie's staff brought out towels and blankets for the three men, since they were visibly shivering.

"We don't have an ID on the body. I put an APB out with a description," the chief said, wrinkles tightening on his face. "With a storm coming on this sudden and intense, we're going to have missing persons."

I shot Elana a quick text that Kirk was here.

Nate and Kirk slumped down into chairs. Nate dried his face with the towel. There was a vacant look in his bloodshot eyes. It was probably shock.

I went back to the kitchen to ask if they had any hot beverages. One of the night staff, Jose, returned with cups of apple cider.

"When I looked out the window of the shed, I saw something caught under a branch." Nate said, a towel around his neck. "I made my way out to him and saw it was an older man, wearing just a t-shirt and jeans. He looked like he'd hit his head on something. I was able to get him out and drag him onto the shore. I tried resuscitating him, but he'd been dead for a while."

Of course. Nate, the Eagle Scout, would do this.

Kirk took a drink of his hot cider and gave Nate a look tinged with awe. "Nate jumped in to save the guy. We almost lost him along with the old man. The pull of the current was so strong. I know *I* couldn't have gotten him back to shore."

"Our John Doe probably went out to check the rising water down river and got swept away," the chief said, reaching for a mug of cider. "But I'm still not sure of the cause of death. I hope to hear from the county coroner sometime tomorrow."

"My photo files and equipment are at the Schiffers now, out of danger." Nate looked tiredly over at Kirk. "Thanks, man."

It's a good feeling when your partner bonds with your best friend's partner. Nate and Kirk hadn't had much interaction before this, but it looked like the experience had brought them together.

The chief toweled his sparse head of wet hair and frowned. "Well, I'm gonna go up and get some sleep. Tomorrow's going to have enough troubles of its own." Then he added wryly under his breath, "Merry Christmas."

He wrapped a blanket around his shoulders like a toga and plodded up the stairs to his room.

"I need to get back to Elana." Kirk's mouth stretched into a yawn. "I'm not getting up early to open gifts, that's for sure."

After he'd left, I leaned over to Nate. "Let's go upstairs."

He looked absolutely exhausted, and water was still dripping down the ends of his hair. There was concern in his light blue eyes. "Is there a shower? I really need a shower."

"There's a shower." I smiled, taking his hand, which felt ice cold. He stood up.

Together, we walked upstairs. Slowly.

⁂

THE NEXT MORNING, I woke to an insistent tap on the door.

I'd slept so soundly that when I first opened my eyes, I didn't realize where I was.

This wasn't my house. But Biga was curled up by my side as usual. And a very large man was laying in the bed next to me, smelling like potpourri body wash.

One of the overnight staff had brought Nate and me some t-shirts and pants she'd found in the lost and found, so we had dry, comfortable clothes to sleep in.

I was thankful for that, even if my sweatpants had Santa Cruz Beach Boardwalk logos—*In the warm, California sun!*—emblazoned all over them, despite the fact that we weren't going to see any of that sun for a week. Nate was essentially sporting capri pants. With his height, the sweatpants from the lost-and-found box hit him mid-calf.

When the tapping continued, I dragged myself out of the bed, extending a foot gingerly down to the floor below.

I opened the door to see Chief Westerman, dressed for business. There were shadows under his eyes, and he looked beat.

I tried to stifle a yawn. "Hi, Dave. Uh . . . merry Christmas."

"I need to talk to Nate." I suspected the chief had heard back from the coroner.

I turned to look at the bed, where Nate was still down for the count, one arm draped over his chest.

"Yes, I see he's asleep." The chief scrolled through a message on his phone. "Tell him I need to talk to him downstairs in the dining room as soon as possible."

I groaned and turned around to assess the state of Nate. I didn't feel like waking him. The guy'd had a hard night.

"I heard him," he said, without opening his eyes. "I'll get up."

"Well, happy Christmas morning," I said after I shut the door. "I hope you got some sleep."

Nate put his feet down on the side of the bed and stood up.

"He'll just have to take me this way," Nate said with a groan as he tried to pull the ends of his sweatpants down to his ankles. "I'm not going to impress anyone today."

"Except *me*," I offered sweetly.

"That's all I care about," he said with a grin, heading for the bathroom.

I wanted to check on how The Laughing Loaf fared during the storm, so I got dressed in yesterday's clothes to go downstairs with him. I took a gulp from my water bottle and then put on some lip gloss and my raincoat. Biga leaped off the bed, skittering as he tried to right himself on the slick hardwood floor.

"Biga boy, you did it." I laughed. I found his leash and snapped it onto his harness. "We need to take a walk in the rain. It's not going to make you happy."

I went to the window and peered through the curtains. The rain had not let up, and water was collecting in puddles on the flat, tarred sections of the roof.

The hundred-year-old bank building that was now my bakery would almost certainly have a few leaks, and I wanted to do what I could to stave off water damage.

At 8:15 a.m., Nate, Biga and I came down the stairs to a

nearly empty dining area. The chief, accompanied by Deputy Brad Castro, had set up a command post at one of the tables. He had a binder open and was typing on his tablet. Next to him, Deputy Brad Castro hunkered over a cup of coffee, looking like he'd had a bad night and didn't want to be here.

Nate pulled me close.

"See you soon," he whispered in my ear, gripping my hand and then letting go. He took a seat across from the chief.

Then the realization hit me. If the chief needed to talk to Nate, the old man's death probably hadn't been an accident.

Reggie, who'd been standing by the kitchen, came out and handed me a dry umbrella.

"Thanks, Reggie. I need to check on the bakery. I suspect we have some leaks."

"I was outside earlier. It's not coming down as hard this morning," he said. "But watch out for the wind. You don't want Biga to blow away."

Biga looked at me in terror. We pushed through the double doors and plunged out into the rain. Biga edged back in the direction of The Riverside and pulled on the leash.

It looked like a tornado had hit downtown River Grove. Clumps of debris lay scattered over the greenspace in front of The Riverside. Branches, paper cups, a tipped-over trash can, a bench plastered with saturated newspapers and a lost pet flyer. Biga stepped around pinecones and trash daintily as we headed for the street.

When we came to the gutter in front of the bakery, Biga stopped. A muddy torrent of water rushed down it. Since he'd be up to his doggy knees in it, I picked him up and carried him.

It wasn't until I opened the door of The Laughing Loaf and walked into the dining area that I realized something: the lights in the dining area and over the front counter were still on. These were lights we left on at night for security purposes.

Wait a minute.

We didn't have a generator that kicked in when the power went out. I knew for sure that most businesses on the street did not have power.

Why did we?

I flipped the switch in the back room, which was nice and tidy after our cleanup yesterday.

Except for a few puddles on the floor. I looked up to see a steady drip coming down from the ceiling in front of the proofer. Several of the floor tiles were beginning to warp.

After setting Biga up in his pen to get him out of my way, I grabbed a large bucket from the storage room and quickly put it in place on the puddle—which would last maybe half a day till it filled up. I'd mop up what I could before I left.

I followed the puddles to the metal table and suddenly felt a steady cold drip on my head akin to water torture. I pulled a large metal bowl from under the table to catch the drip.

After mopping up as best I could, I looked around for other signs of leaks or flooding. Surprisingly, the bakery seemed relatively unscathed.

If we continued having power, maybe my bakery could help the town out. I could bake for our neighbors, those who couldn't bake for themselves. Or supply them with hot coffee. Or just give them a warm place to hang out.

"Okay, Biga." I went in to retrieve my little dog from his pen. "Let's get back to Reggie's place."

Biga put his paws up on the gate and clamored to get out. I lifted him up and decided to spare him from getting his paws wet by carrying him.

Back at The Riverside, Nate and the chief were still at the table in the dining area, but they were talking casually now.

I invited myself to join them and took a seat next to Nate, Biga in my lap.

"We've identified the man in the river," the chief said, after a sip of coffee. "I knew of the man but didn't recognize him last night. His name's Randall Sterlin. I went to check on him yesterday, by his daughter's request, but I saw no signs of anyone in his cabin. He lived up the river, outside town. He kept to himself." The chief picked up a carton of milk and dumped a liberal amount in his mug.

Biga was on my lap giving such longing looks at my boyfriend, I finally handed him over to Nate.

"What did the coroner say about how he died?"

The chief took in his breath. "Well, that's why I wanted to ask Nate questions about the condition of the body. The coroner said his head wound was caused by a blunt instrument—a hammer or axe handle—not something he'd likely have gotten from falling into the river."

Who'd have killed an old man who kept to himself? On Christmas Eve?

"No other friends or relatives in the area?" I asked.

The chief shook his head. "Corinne told me he worked for the county as a surveyor. Bought some land with his earnings when he retired and built the cabin by himself. He was always on the lookout for trespassers and kept a shotgun handy. The mayor said she saw him at a few town meetings, whenever the subject of land rights came up. He would angrily share his point of view, then leave."

If Randall Sterlin had been living in town for years, I wondered if Beck and her family knew him. She seemed to know everyone and be friendly with everyone, even people as reclusive as Randall Sterlin.

"Did you check the cabin out yourself when you went over yesterday?" I asked the chief, who frowned. I didn't mean it to sound like I was stepping on his turf. The chief tended to get defensive about these things. Nate gave me an assessing look, probably concerned I was going to do what I usually do, jump into the case.

"When I went over yesterday, it looked like someone had trashed the place." He eyed me warily, then sighed. "I'm heading back after this. Want to come with me? I'm taking my Jeep, since the terrain is wet and a little unstable."

I caught Nate's eye, since I didn't want to take off and leave him if he wanted to spend time with me. I mean, it *was* Christmas Day.

He pulled my hand up and kissed it. "You go ahead. I'll take Biga upstairs with me. I could use a couple more hours of sleep."

As the chief and I prepared to leave, my dad and Mary Jo came down and joined Nate at the table. They hadn't heard about the events of last night. I telegraphed a look to Nate: *go now*. He needed to get upstairs before my dad started talking to him—or challenged him to what would certainly be multiple games of chess.

I hugged Mary Jo and wished her and my dad a happy Christmas. I still had presents upstairs for everyone that I hadn't given out last night. I wanted to have a proper Christmas when we got back.

As rain continued to pelt the jeep, the chief pulled out

of the saloon's parking lot, and we took the highway heading east out of town. After about three miles, he turned onto a dirt road, saturated by the rains. Fifty feet in on the road, we sank down into mud. The chief gunned the engine for a couple of minutes. He swore under his breath and pounded on the wheel. Then he got out and wedged some wood under the tires. After a few tries, we lurched out onto firmer ground.

"Hey, I checked on the bakery this morning. We never lost power. Do you know why that would be?" I braced myself with one hand on the dashboard as we bumped along on the uneven road, through a thick grove of trees.

The chief answered me, still focused on the rugged terrain ahead of us. "That's because you're on the power grid for essential services, along with city hall."

"Wait a minute." I laughed. "My *bakery* is on the power grid for essential services?"

"We're on it since we're police and city services. You're on it because your building used to be the old Bank of River Grove."

So that explained it. I liked that baking cinnamon rolls and bread had become an essential service.

"Since I have power, I want to help people. Serve fresh bread and coffee–make it a meeting place for people in town."

The chief nodded. "People could use your Wi-Fi and check in with friends and relatives. That will be helpful, as long as people can *get* to downtown. I've already heard of two roads washed out in the hills."

We pulled off the road onto an even less defined narrow gravel road, more like a path—also muddy. A small cabin made of stained wood sat at the end of the path.

When we got out, I pulled my rain hat down over my

head. On top of the pounding rain, I heard the powerful rush of the river on the other side of Randall Sterlin's cabin. Before the storm, the San Luciano River gurgled as it flowed over rocks beyond our house's back fence. Today, the same river next to Randall Sterlin's house roared.

The chief pulled open the screen door then opened the unlocked front door to the house. I followed him inside.

Randall Sterlin's place was tiny—a small kitchen, a living room and what looked like a bedroom-bathroom off to our right. The place smelled of mildew. It was furnished simply and looked like it had probably been kept fairly neat.

That is, until somebody pulled drawers out of the desk in his living room and the bedroom dresser and dumped the contents onto the floor.

The chief took out his phone and moved through the house, taking pictures of each room.

I walked into the kitchen to see cupboards open, jars smashed, and pots across the floor. Scattered among the debris were shiny nickels and dimes.

"Someone was looking for something," I called out to the chief, as I gingerly stepped across the littered tile floor. "And they apparently found a lot of loose change."

"Oh, yeah, the mayor told me Sterlin collected things— coins and stamps." The chief picked up a fireplace poker and used it to root through the area near the desk. "He took his collections to local shows to buy and sell."

"Maybe someone wanted his collections. Were they worth much?" I asked, as I opened up the back door, which led to a side yard and another menacing view of the swollen river.

The chief called from the desk in the living room. "I wouldn't think so. Sounds like he was a small-time collector. It was something to keep him busy."

The deadbolt on the back door was unlocked. I pulled a paper towel off the roll on the counter and used it to open the door to avoid leaving prints.

"Chief, the back door's not locked." I pulled the door open and got hit in the face with cold, sideways rain.

"Just a minute, Gracie." The chief met me in the kitchen. He stepped over the debris and examined the door. "He could have been attacked when he stepped out back."

If Nate had found the man wearing just a t-shirt and jeans, it sounded like Sterlin had been caught unawares. He hadn't prepped for a walk outside in the storm. I looked out towards the churning river, and saw a rough trail down to the river bank, now muddy and littered with branches,.

"Who would go out in a storm like this to attack an old man?" I pulled my raincoat up around my neck and stepped onto the small, concrete back porch.

"Whatever they came for, they got away without attracting any attention. Nobody's going to be outside in a storm like this, especially not in this area. They could kill him and take what they wanted."

"Was he the kind of guy who'd keep his nest egg under his mattress?" I looked back into the cabin's disarray. "If he was distrustful of banks, maybe he kept all his money here. Somebody took advantage of the storm to take his stash."

"You could be right." The chief nodded as he looked at two glasses sitting in the sink. "I don't know a lot about Sterlin, but I do know he didn't trust the government *or* banks."

"Poor guy," I said, walking back into the house. "What happens now?"

The chief leaned against the kitchen counter. He took out his phone. "I'll talk with his daughter and son-in-law. I need to know more about the man's habits. Like whether he did keep his money in the cabin."

"Did he have friends in town?" I asked, glancing at a pile of mail on the kitchen counter. I noticed the return address on one: *American Numismatist*, based in Pollard Creek, Arizona.

"I can ask his daughter, but I don't recall who he was close with these days. Way back, I heard he, Rod Heston, and some of the old-timers in town were buddies."

Rod Heston was April Lewis's grandfather, a River Grove native, someone I'd had some tense interactions with last year when I was investigating the murder of April's rock star father. I'm pretty sure Heston blamed me for his life being dramatically turned upside down after that.

"You don't think he and his friends stayed in touch?"

The chief shrugged as he poked through a pile of debris on the living room floor. "From what I heard, Sterlin barricaded himself up here and didn't get out much. If you're curious, talk to Rod."

With parts of town blocked off and phone service out for a lot of our town's inhabitants, that wasn't likely to happen anytime soon.

The chief pulled out a couple of pairs of latex gloves and handed me one, then pulled his on. He'd just stooped down to go through a drawer of papers, mail, and receipts that had been pulled out onto the floor, when I heard a cracking noise.

"Damn knee," he muttered, then went to the kitchen and brought back a chair. He plopped down on it and bent down to root through the pile.

"You okay, chief?"

"Yes, it happens when you get old. I'm *fine*." He grunted in annoyance, then turned up the corner of his mouth in a weary smile. "Just you wait, kiddo."

Most of the drawer's contents looked like mail, though I

saw what looked like a hanging folder, stuffed with weathered papers. When the chief picked it up, there was a smudged brown spot on the green carpet underneath. I eyed it with interest.

"Is that blood?"

The chief leaned over in his chair to peer down at it. He snapped a photo of it on his phone. He laid a sheet of paper down on it and pressed. He pulled the paper up to reveal an imprint of the brownish spot. "Fairly recent. If he was killed in the house, there should be more."

I peered into the bedroom, right off the living room. There was a neatly made bed and an unvarnished dresser topped by what looked like a cow skull. Its drawers were pulled out, and the contents strewn over the bedroom floor. Next to the bed stood a nightstand with a few historical books: a hefty biography of George Washington and a paperback called *The Intolerable Acts: America's Road to Revolution.*

I retraced my path to the kitchen, looking for more. When I got to the back door again, I noticed odd-looking brown streaks on the linoleum, like an imprint made by something wrinkled or folded. I opened the door and looked out to the surging river a little more than fifteen feet from the door. I wondered how long it would take for the rising river to get to the back steps. It might not be long before much of the small cabin was flooded, destroying any evidence. If there were clues here as to who'd killed Sterlin, we'd have to find them soon.

Rain came down hard and the wind was playing with a sheet of plastic in the backyard near the river. It tumbled across the yard and eventually the wind flattened it against a redwood tree near the riverbank. It looked like a shower curtain.

I pictured the killer attacking Sterlin in the house, then dragging him down to the river on it.

As I looked across the raging river, I was startled to see a man watching me, someone barely visible walking beyond the trees. The man looked at me, then quickly disappeared into the blur of rain and trees.

When I came back inside, the chief was still sitting on his chair. He filled an evidence envelope with some papers as he went through the desk drawer. He stood up and went over to the kitchen counter to grab the unopened mail. He pulled out what looked like a bank statement and turned it over in his hands.

"The killer probably took anything of value with him." The chief sat back in his chair and looked up at me. "But there's a tablet of paper here. A page had been torn off, so I ran a pencil over the blank page to see if I could read the imprint." He held up the pad of paper. The word revealed from the impression read LIBERTY! All capital letters and an exclamation mark.

This might turn the investigation in another direction. Was Sterlin involved in some kind of a militia movement? It wasn't unusual to find in remote locations like this. He was anti-government. I did notice the pantry next to the kitchen was stocked with 20-pound bags of rice. The shelves were lined with stacks of canned beans, mandarin oranges, and pineapple rings. Gallon water containers stood at the ready.

"Was he a survivalist?" I asked. I wanted to ask the chief if I could open Sterlin's mail on the counter, but I figured the answer would be "no" and I'd get a lecture, so I didn't bother.

"It wouldn't surprise me if Sterlin was involved in a movement like that," the chief said as he bent down to pick up an opened envelope from the drawer. "He was a loner with very strong ideas, most of them opposing local government.”

What was there was to rebel against in friendly little River Grove?

As I knelt down and started pawing through the papers on the floor, I wondered how much we'd be able to investigate Randall Sterlin's murder today.

For one, it was Christmas Day. We may or may not have internet service, though I could probably get online at The Laughing Loaf or The Riverside. When I tried to google something on my phone here at Sterlin's, I got a *no internet service* message.

“I have to get back to City Hall,” the chief said, rising with a grunt from his chair. “At least I can make phone calls and search the databases there.”

“I'd like to see if Heston has any ideas on what Sterlin was up to.” I buttoned my raincoat and wrapped the scarf around my neck, tucking it into my hood. “I'll try to reach him through April Lewis. Not sure he'll talk to me.”

The chief tilted his head and nodded. “He probably wouldn't give me the time of day either. He had a rough time after Noah Thornton Bell's murder.” The chief slipped the evidence packet into a plastic bag, then slid it into his case. He looked up at me. “Rod's not a bad man, Gracie.”

Maybe.

I'd heard that from Rod's daughter, Angie, and his granddaughter, April. Rod Heston came across as a grumpy old man. He'd had a rotten year. But apart from a serious grudge against rockstar Noah Thornton Bell, he hadn't really done anything to deserve his life falling apart.

All packed, the chief and I headed back to the jeep,

hunched over and pushing against the wind as the rain beat down, stinging our faces.

I took one last look at the river, sloshing up over the bank. I wondered how long it would be till Sterlin's house flooded.

After our slow, bumpy journey back to the highway nearly trapped us again in the mud, we pulled up to my house on Pilgrim Way. I wanted to check the condition of our property.

When I stepped out of the car, the first thing I heard was the river, louder than I'd ever heard it in our time in River Grove.

I dodged sheets of rain to get to my front door. Inside, I shoved clothes for me and my dad into a large trash bag and grabbed Biga's dog food. When I passed our hallway mirror, I groaned at my hair, which the rain and wind had tossed into a wet, curly mass. Nate said he liked it this way, but it felt out of control to me.

As I looked out the back window of our house, the river had risen over its banks, but it didn't look like it would endanger our house—yet. A fallen tree had taken out a chunk of our back fence.

"Any damage?" The chief asked when I got back in the Jeep.

"The river doesn't seem to be threatening the house at this point. There's a tree down on our fence."

"People in town are dealing with much worse, Gracie."

A sobering thought. I knew Mary Jo would have a lot of cleanup to do at Growing Affection.

Once we got back to the Riverside and warmed up with apple cider, the chief pulled an umbrella from the stand by the saloon's double doors.

"Now that this is a murder case, I'm heading back to

City Hall. Deputy Brad and I will go through the papers and photos and see what we can find out. I have a few more questions for Sterlin's daughter."

I went upstairs to the room to hang my wet coat near the heater and change into a warm sweater. Nate lay across the bed, completely out of it, one arm flung off the side of the bed with Biga wedged in next to him.

I planted a kiss on Nate's forehead. He didn't even stir.

I sat down at one of the long tables, where my father was playing chess with Reggie McFerrin.

A pile of chess pieces had accumulated on Reggie's side. My dad's brow was furrowed in thought as he leaned forward in his seat.

Reggie was the only chess player in River Grove who could beat my dad.

And my dad loved it.

He spent hours dissecting their games, analyzing the moves to pinpoint how the saloon owner had beat him. I didn't have much interest in these details, but I loved watching my Dad get that excited about losing.

After finishing a move, Reggie turned to me, interest in his eyes. "Gracie, find anything at the cabin?" Then I remembered—if anyone else was likely to know Randall, it was Reggie. He'd been in River Grove since he started his commune here in the 1970s.

"Reggie, did you know Randall Sterlin very well?"

My dad leaned over the chessboard, finger on his chin, as he tried to figure out his next move.

A faint smile crossed Reggie's face. "I remember when he and his wife, Eileen, moved to town. This was before their daughter was born. They came here for the music, mostly because of Eileen. She was a party girl."

"Very different than Randall then," I said, hoping he'd tell me more.

"They were a bad match, but he loved that woman. She left Randall and their little girl when Jennifer was ten. That was when Randall's world began to shrink. Back then, they lived in town. Jenny had her school friends and as soon as she could, she got a job and moved out. Randall became a hermit after that."

I imagined the man trying to barricade himself by withdrawing from society. Hit by his losses and trying to protect what he had left.

"He became very bitter." Reggie looked down at the board and moved a pawn. My dad leaned forward.

"*Aha!*" My dad proclaimed triumphantly and took the pawn with his knight. He waved it around like a toddler who'd just stolen a piece of candy.

I wasn't surprised to hear this about Sterlin, but it didn't help my Christmas cheer. I felt sad for him. I wondered who could have entered this man's tight, little world on Christmas Eve. And why they'd killed him.

"Thanks, Reggie. Do you know anything about Sterlin's friends? The chief said he was friends with Rod Heston."

"That was years ago." Reggie quickly moved his bishop out of the path of my father's oncoming queen. "I'm not sure they stayed in touch."

I sat down next to my dad and pulled out my phone to text April Lewis.

> Merry Christmas! Hope you're having fun with your Aunt Corrie today. Got time to chat?

A few minutes later, my phone buzzed.

By Victoria Kazarian

OMG GRACIE. I SO need to get out.

Meet me at The Laughing Loaf. We have power.

See you in 20!

I went upstairs to get Biga on a leash and take him outside to get a pee break and go to the bakery with me. He was trying to burrow under the comforter to get closer to Nate. Finally, I sneaked up on him. I snapped the leash onto his collar when he wasn't looking and slipped on his blue, down dog jacket, which he was not a fan of.

Chloe Westerman wandered downstairs not long after us. She didn't look like she'd slept much last night. She had dark circles under her lively eyes.

She grabbed a granola bar from the table and ripped it open. "I'm going stir crazy. I'm sick of hanging out with my mom. And my grandfather. He says The Laughing Loaf still has power. You going over?"

"I was just about to meet up with April Lewis."

"Oh! I'd love to see her." Working for The Laughing Loaf on an as-needed basis had hooked Chloe on baking, especially anything sweet. "Think I could bake something while we're there?"

"Let's check to see everything's working. If it is, sure."

Chloe grabbed her coat from the table and pulled her hood up over her head.

As we headed toward the door, Biga looked up at me with big, sad eyes.

He knew wet paws were in his future.

·   ·   ·

W E S H O O K ourselves off on the mat after coming through the Laughing Loaf's front door and set our umbrellas in the stand.

It felt good to get back to my bakery, and I was excited for the friends meetup. Biga willingly walked back to his pen. He must have missed it. He curled up on his blanket, happy to be in a familiar place.

The drip pots I'd put out were nearly full. Chloe helped me empty them, then she started up the espresso machine to make the three of us drinks. The familiar sound and smell made me salivate.

"It doesn't feel like The Laughing Loaf without Beck," Chloe said as she handed me a latte.

I nodded. "I just saw her yesterday, but it seems like years, doesn't it? Nate told me he heard from Sam. The road up to her parents' house is still blocked by a tree."

"Hopefully her brothers clear it with their chainsaws soon," Chloe said as she sipped her latte. "I miss that girl."

April Lewis came in the front door completely soaked, her wet, pink hair plastered against her forehead.

"Sorry I'm late. I'd give you both a hug but look at me." She rolled her eyes.

"I want to hear about your tour with the Hooting Heathers," I said as we gathered around a table away from the windows. I didn't want anyone passing by to think we were open for business yet.

We sat drinking coffee in the nice warm dining area as April talked about concerts she'd played with her bluegrass band all over Europe—from a tiny club in London to a bier-garten in Germany.

"What was your favorite place?" Chloe asked, her chin leaning on her hand, her face wistful. I had a feeling she'd want to spend her summer after graduating from high school traveling—which would make the chief sad. He was trying hard to improve his relationship with her in the short time he had before she left for college.

"Ooooh. Let me see. Italy was so cool." April's eyes glowed and she leaned across the table as she emphasized her words. "I mean, the *food,* you guys. They have this drink called limoncello that's the most amazing thing I've ever tasted."

Chloe asked lots of questions about the cities April had seen then excused herself to bake a pan of cinnamon rolls in the back room.

"April, how's it going with your grandfather?"

"We had dinner together at The Riverside the night before Christmas Eve. I wasn't super excited about doing it, but it was good. Grandpa Rod was so chill. He listened a lot. He didn't trash talk my dad, so that was good. Mostly we talked about the tour and my mom. My mom didn't want my grandparents to be in my life, and I totally get that. I guess my dad did some bad things in River Grove when he was growing up."

This was a change in April. Earlier this year, she'd defended her dad fiercely, refusing to believe anything negative about him. Noah Thornton Bell, like all people, had been a mixed bag: part juvenile delinquent, part loyal friend. An unscrupulous band leader, yet a loving dad, who'd given his talented daughter her start in the music business. Maybe she was beginning to see him more realistically.

"April, do you think your grandfather would talk to me? One of his old friends was murdered yesterday. I'd like to ask Rod some questions about him."

April shrugged. "I think he'd be okay. It's not like he blames you for what happened with my dad's case. I brought up your name at dinner. He didn't spit on the ground or anything."

I sat back in my chair and snorted. "Okay, that's encouraging. Do you think you could tell him that I'd like to chat with him about Randall Sterlin?"

"His house is within walking distance, so maybe he could meet you here or at The Riverside. I'll tell him you'd like to talk."

This was way more than I'd hoped for.

After a lot more gabbing, giggling, and another round of lattes, we ate some of Chloe's fresh-from-the-oven cinnamon rolls. Before Chloe and April left, we took a group selfie to send to Beck, who at this point may or may not have had any connection to the outside world.

Since the chief and I both had access to the internet, I texted him and asked if he'd like to come over to the bakery for coffee. I wanted to hear if he'd found out any more about Randall Sterlin from the man's daughter and son-in-law. And, to be honest, I was trying to work up enough courage to talk to Rod Heston.

I looked up to see the chief crossing the street in the pouring rain just ten minutes later. He must have been desperate for good coffee.

I let him in the front door then started in on making his latte.

He guzzled the stuff like I'd handed him a glass of water in the desert. He sank down in his seat with a satisfied sigh.

"I found out a little more about Sterlin's activities. Corinne told me he and his friends were planning to set up a compound not far from Sterlin's cabin. They were going to declare it independent territory, free from any form of government."

"Is that even a thing?" I shook my head.

"I'm pretty sure it isn't," the chief said, taking a gulp of his latte. "But this is a group of River Grove old timers who have an axe to grind."

"I can see where Sterlin would be drawn to like minds."

"Corinne thinks he put all his money into the plan. I read his bank statement." The chief leveled his eyes at me. "Sterlin had a hell of a lot more money than I thought."

"The man was living on rice and canned beans. We saw his pantry. How much could he have?"

The chief shook his head.

"He wasn't keeping it under his mattress, Gracie. As of last month, he had three million dollars in his bank accounts."

Chapter Five

I really needed to talk to Rod Heston.

At the same time, it was Christmas Day.

My boyfriend, my dad, and my dad's girlfriend were back at The Riverside. We had gifts to exchange.

"April thinks her father would talk to me. She said he was 'chill' now."

The chief tilted his head. "Huh. Guess we'll find out soon."

I'd wait to see if I heard from Rod Heston. Meanwhile, I'd get myself and my little dog back to The Riverside, for more of Reggie's guac and chips and maybe some of those delicious desserts I'd missed last night.

Biga and I came back with the half-eaten pan of Chloe's cinnamon rolls and shared them with Reggie and my dad, who were still discussing the details of Reggie's chess win.

Mary Jo and I sat and picked at cinnamon rolls while talking about something a lot more interesting to us: family Christmas traditions we remembered as children. I told her about my mother's and my tradition of getting eggnog lattes during our Christmas shopping and how my mother played

Silent Night on Christmas morning to signal it was time to open presents.

Mary Jo told me about growing up in Arizona, and her town's Hispanic tradition of Las Posadas, in which children reenacted Joseph's and Mary's journey, going from house to house to find a place to stay before Jesus's birth.

When Reggie got up and headed back to the kitchen to talk to the staff about dinner, I stood up.

"I'd better wake Nate. I've got gifts for everyone."

"I'll get my gifts, too." Mary Jo said excitedly, standing up.

I headed for the stairs. Then I heard a familiar voice call out my name.

I looked over to see Rod Heston standing by the double doors. He wore a bright yellow rain slicker. With his leathery, timeworn face, he looked a little like the Gorton fisherman, fresh off an Atlantic trawler.

He also looked like he wasn't at all excited to talk to me.

Trying to keep my nervousness at bay, I went over to greet him.

"April said you wanted to ask me about Randall Sterlin." His face, with its sharp features looked twisted, whether out of grief or out of having to talk to me, I didn't know. "Where can we talk?"

We took a table at the far end of the dining hall. He took off his slicker and laid it over a chair.

"Thank you for coming here," I started in. "I know it's been a hard year for you, Rod, with the arrest. And I'm so sorry."

He shook his head. "It ain't your fault, Gracie. I've had me some blessings in this rotten year. I'm spending time with my granddaughter for the first time. We're getting along pretty good."

"I'm glad for you." I nodded and smiled. "And I really appreciate you coming over. The chief said you were friends with Randall. Unfortunately, sometime yesterday, he was murdered. I wanted to ask you about him."

Rod looked down at the table and scratched the back of his neck. "Yeah, I didn't see Randall very often over the past ten years. A few months ago, we rekindled things. We started talking."

"I heard he was in a group that was buying land to build a compound." I told him. "They wanted to start their own government."

Rod thought for a moment. "I don't know nothing about that, though I guess it could be true. He didn't like what the county and the town were doing with his land."

"What do you mean?" I asked, settling back in my seat, since this might be a long talk. "Was there something they did that he disagreed with?"

"It was his house." Rod frowned. "The county wouldn't give him a permit to build on his own land. They said it was too close to the river. He couldn't build legally."

I remembered the river surging over its bank, edging closer to Sterlin's back door by the hour. The county was right.

"Randall built it anyway?"

Rod raised his hand in a gesture of emphasis. "He damn well did. Built it himself. He said the county and the city had no right to tell him what to do. So, when they said they was going to condemn his house, he went to the town meetings and told them to go to hell."

This did not surprise me. "So how involved was he in this anti-government group? Mayor C said his daughter tried to talk him out of giving them his money."

Rod narrowed his eyes and gave me a skeptical look.

"You gotta know this—Jennifer hated her daddy. She blamed him for her mama leaving. She moved out as soon as she turned eighteen and didn't look back. Then Randy told me he'd talked to her maybe twice in the past month."

Something was off here.

"Let me ask you something." I leaned over the table. "The chief found a bank statement that said Randall had about three million dollars in his accounts. Maybe he saved his salary from working for the county for years, and maybe he was living off beans and rice. But it wouldn't amount to *that* much. Do you know where he could have gotten that much money?"

Rod sat back in his seat, a grim look on his face.

"Yeah. I think I might."

I'D CALLED the chief downstairs to continue the conversation with Rod. He'd just woken up. He padded down the stairs in a robe, jeans, and a t-shirt, and a pair of ancient, battered slippers.

I suspected the chief was just as uncomfortable as I was about talking to Rod again. But he slumped down at the table, set down his glass of orange juice, and greeted the River Grove old timer with a handshake.

"Good to see you, Rod. Thank you for being willing to talk about Randall."

Rod gave him a curt nod. "I think someone's done my old friend wrong. If I can do anything to help, I will."

The Chief leveled a serious look at Rod. "You told Gracie that Randall and his daughter hadn't talked in years. Is this true?"

Rod nodded. "Yes, sir. Until last month. Jennifer

wanted nothing to do with her daddy. He didn't wanna talk to her neither."

The chief let out a sigh. "That's not what I heard from her. She said she loved her dad and was very worried about him." He shook his head. "Fact is, Rod, there's something fishy here. I found a bank statement in his cabin that surprised the hell out of me."

Rod folded his hands together over the table. "When I talked to Randy, he told me things were changing for him. He could afford to hire a lawyer. He wanted to fight the city and the county for the right to live in his house."

Something was clear to me. Randall Sterlin stubbornly clung to things that weren't good for him. He lived for years with a woman who couldn't stand him, who'd finally left him. And he'd built his house dangerously close to the river —then fought the city for the right to live in it.

Rod continued. "The last time I saw Randall, he asked me to go to his lawyer's office with him. He said he didn't trust nobody, but he did trust me. He made me trustee of his estate."

For a moment, I remembered my past suspicions about Rod Heston. After this summer's investigation into the death of Noah Bell, Rod had come off looking innocent—a caring father and grandfather. What if that wasn't entirely true? Rod wasn't well off in his dilapidated cottage at the edge of town. I wondered if Sterlin's offer to make him trustee of his millions was too much of a temptation for Rod. I tried to set this aside and focus on the facts of the situation.

"So you know more than we do, Rod," I said, tapping my feet under the table impatiently. "Where did Sterlin get that money?"

"He'd found something—a coin he bought at a show in

Sacramento. The kid who sold it to him didn't know now much it was worth. But Randy did. He bought it for fifty bucks and the kid went away thinking *he* got a deal. Randy read that this coin had been missing for a long time. Some people didn't think it existed." He snorted and shook his head. "It was a *nickel*. Randy sold it for almost three million dollars."

"By any chance, did he have a name for it?" I asked.

"He told me it was called 'Liberty,'" Rod said.

I sucked in my breath. The word that appeared on the notepad when the chief scrawled over it in pencil.

After this revelation from Rod, it was going to be hard for me to stay focused on Christmas or on the storm still raging outside. I'd be picking away at the puzzle.

This hadn't been some burglar who'd raided random cabins during the storm to see what they could get.

Randall Sterlin had been murdered by someone who knew he'd just come into a fortune.

WHILE NATE HUNG out downstairs with my dad and Mary Jo, I snuggled under the quilt in the four-poster bed upstairs and used The Riverside's excellent internet connection to gorge myself on every bit of information I could find about the 1913 Liberty Head Nickel.

Nate came upstairs with Biga in his arms, to see how I was doing. He found Biga's leash on the dresser.

"I can tell you're in the zone," he said with an amused look in his eyes. "The rain's supposed to let up in a few minutes. I'm going to take Biga out for a walk."

"He'll fight you, you know. He hates the rain."

"Our diva will have to deal with it," Nate said, snapping

the leash onto Biga's collar. "Oh, and I just found out gift-giving has been pushed to after dinner, so you've got a couple of hours."

He bent down to give me a kiss, as Biga gave me a nervous look.

After Nate left and shut the door, I leaned back on the pillows and listened to the patter of rain on the window. The wind had let up, and the steady drops sounded calming.

Now to come up with a plan to trap Randall Sterlin's killer.

☙

At 2 p.m., my phone buzzed with a text.

It was the chief.

> New info about Sterlin. Meet me in my office.

Crawling reluctantly out of my warm bed, I slipped on boots and grabbed my wool coat. With a wave to Reggie in the main hall, I dashed down the street to city hall, trying to avoid the puddles forming in the road's potholes.

The Chief met me at the back entrance of city hall.

He opened the door and escorted me down to his office in the hallway.

"Turns out I have a very helpful daughter," he said with a crooked smile as we walked. "Renee has a friend who works at Sterlin's bank, First National in Santa Cruz."

As we entered the chief's office, I saw Renee Wester-man, sitting confidently at her father's desk, dressed in neat slacks and a tailored jacket, seemingly untouched by the rain. She looked as if she were CEO of City Hall, Inc.

She stood up to greet me when I came in.

"Hi, Gracie. When my dad told me what had happened, I called my friend Linda Machado at the bank. Here, why don't you have a seat?" She got up and pulled a chair over for me to sit in, while the chief looked around his office forlornly for seating. "She's a supervisor there. She said Randall came in with his daughter Jennifer on December 20 and made a big, six-figure transfer to her account. The customer representative said Sterlin looked very uncomfortable, and she suspected he was making the transfer under duress. Linda called county adult protective services to report it as elder abuse."

I exchanged glances with the chief. "So she had seen her father recently. And she must have found out about his big sale."

The chief nodded. "I'm sure of it."

"We need to get her down here," I said. "Maybe lure her here by saying we found something else of Sterlin's that might be worth something. Since she's his next of kin, you thought she'd be interested in keeping it."

"It's worth a try," the chief said with a shrug. After a stern look at his daughter, she vacated his desk chair.

The chief made his call.

His lips twisted almost mischievously as he told Sterlin's daughter he'd found a bag of coins that might be worth something. He wanted to make sure she knew about them, since she was his next of kin. And with the current storm, her father's house would be under water very soon.

"So we'll see you and your husband soon. I'm sorry about your father's *accident*, Mrs. McCord."

About forty minutes later, Jennifer and her husband Doug arrived at city hall's back entrance.

The two were dressed in what looked like brand-new

clothes. Jennifer wore a white pantsuit, with gold ankle boots and a long coat that looked like it was made out of light brown fur. Doug wore a black suit and tie with a gold money clip.

Shortly after entering the chief's office, Jennifer took a tissue out of her purse and began dabbing at her eyes.

"I can't believe he's gone," she said, sniffing into a tissue she pulled out of her handbag. "My daddy died so *alone*."

Doug sat stiffly next to his wife, nodding distractedly. He looked like he wanted to be anywhere else.

"Jennifer, when we searched your father's cabin, we found this." On the desk, the chief set down a linen bag of coins he'd collected from the floor of Sterlin's kitchen.

Jennifer's eyes widened with excitement as they locked onto the bag. "Do you know how much they're worth?"

The chief shook his head. "We aren't sure. But your father had a good sense of how valuable these things were."

Jennifer couldn't stop staring at the bag. She reached for it and weighed it speculatively in one hand.

"He sure did," she breathed.

"We also found something else in the cabin—a bank statement listing your father's account at three million dollars."

Then Renee spoke up. "I talked to his banker at First National today, Jennifer. She said you came in and had your father transfer $800,000 to your account. He did not look happy to be doing it. In fact, she said he looked downright scared. She filed an elder abuse report with the county."

Jennifer looked terrified. Doug looked uneasy.

"What are you saying?" Jennifer said indignantly. "My father *gave* me that money. Because he felt guilty for being a crappy dad."

"You knew about your father's coin collecting hobby,

and when you read about someone in River Grove selling a very rare nickel, you knew exactly who it was," I said. "You threatened your father. Told him you'd turn him in to the county and make sure they destroyed his house—unless he gave you a share of the money."

Jennifer's face reddened with anger. She looked to her husband for support, but he wasn't giving any.

"What happened, Jennifer? Did your father say he wasn't going to transfer you any more money?" The chief asked calmly. "Is that when you went to his cabin to kill him?"

Beads of sweat formed on Jennifer's forehead. She glanced at her phone. "We have to catch a plane to Vegas in two hours. We don't have time for this."

She grabbed her handbag and turned to her husband, who visibly pulled away from her. "Let's go. *Now*."

He gave her a look of sad resignation. "It's over, babe."

With that, Jennifer Sterlin McCord made a run for the door in her sparkling boots. Renee Westerman, who'd been watching the woman's movements, went after her, catching her arm before she fled into the hallway. As Renee held the woman's arms, the chief calmly came over and snapped handcuffs on Jennifer, then Doug.

"Jennifer McCord, Doug McCord," he said solemnly. "You are under arrest for the murder of Randall Sterlin."

Chapter Six

That Christmas evening, the chief, Mayor C, Reggie, my father and Mary Jo, and Nate and I sat in front of the fireplace in The Riverside's decorated main room. After a big dinner of buffet leftovers from Reggie's commercial fridge and lots of opened gifts, we drank hot toddies and cocoa and warmed ourselves.

"So, what is this liberty head nickel?" My father asked as he sipped a hot toddy. "Who would spend that much money to buy a nickel?"

I told them what I'd found out.

"You've seen buffalo nickels, right?" The older people in the group, including the chief and Mary Jo, nodded at the memory. "They started minting them in 1913, to replace the Liberty Head nickel. After they started making them, a few Liberty Head nickels were pressed, probably by workers at the mint on the sly—even though they weren't supposed to be making them anymore."

"And *that's* why they're worth so much?" Mary Jo asked, a puzzled look on her face.

"Apparently rare pressings are a big deal in the coin

world." I took a sip of spicy Mexican hot chocolate. "So five of those coins, but probably six, went out into the world. Five of those are owned by collectors or on display, and the worth of each is estimated between $3–4 million. There were rumors of a sixth Liberty Head nickel, but nobody had come forth saying they had it. Somehow, that sixth nickel made it into Sterlin's hands."

I continued, based on what the chief had told me after the arrest. "Randall's daughter read about rumors of the rare coin being sold by a collector in River Grove. She figured out it was Sterlin and forced him to make a transfer. When he told Jennifer and Doug he wasn't giving them more, they probably killed him after the storm started on Christmas Eve. I'm sure it was tricky to get to River Grove in that weather. But with everyone sheltering, they did it without being noticed."

"Poor Randall," Mary Jo said sadly, leaning against my dad. He gave her a peck on the cheek.

I looked down at my phone and saw a text message from Beck. It was a classic Beck text, and I was feeling so raw from the events of the past two days, I wanted to cry.

> I got your picture! What a great selfie of you all! I love you guys SO MUCH!!!!!! 🤍 🤍 🤍

> My brothers cleared the tree. We drive home tomorrow. Want to meet at Laughing Loaf?

> WE SO NEED TO BAKE!!!

I rested my head on Nate's arm and laughed to myself.

. . .

THE STORM WOULD STAY with us, just as Reggie and county emergency services predicted. The rain, the falling trees, the power outages, and the washed-out roads would plague River Grove till New Year's Eve.

As the rain and wind began to let up, Beck and I would open The Laughing Loaf for three days. We made hot coffee for everyone and let the power-less citizens of River Grove come in to charge their phones. We'd give away many loaves of warm, freshly baked bread and cinnamon rolls.

A few days later, while we were back in our homes and the storm had moved on, Randall's blood was found on an axe handle in Jennifer and Doug McCord's garage. Tests would also show traces of his blood on the shower curtain found near the river.

Nature—in the intensity of this violent storm—could not match the cruelty of human beings toward other human beings. The world was full of greed and destruction, and I remembered sadly this was not the first time I'd seen it.

But that night, as I sat by Reggie's Christmas fire, all I thought about was how happy I was to be with these people, in this place—enjoying the peace and warmth of a Merry Christmas.

the end

Thank you

Thank you for reading
Gingerbread and Left for Dead!
If you've enjoyed this short holiday mystery, please leave a
review on Amazon, Goodreads, or the book review site of
your choice.

Also by Victoria Kazarian

Drop Dead Bread - Laughing Loaf Mystery #1

Bread to Rights - Laughing Loaf Mystery #2

Trouble You Don't Knead - Laughing Loaf Mystery #3

Sourdough & Cyanide - Laughing Loaf Mystery #4

Proof of Death - Laughing Loaf Mystery #5

An Oven Beyond - Laughing Loaf Mystery #6

Shot Through the Tart - Laughing Loaf Mystery #7

Naan the Wiser - Laughing Loaf Mystery #8

Stop, Drop and Rolls: A Laughing Loaf Bakery Short Mystery
(prequel novella)

**Stay tuned for Laughing Loaf #9 - Rye or Die,
coming soon!**

TRADITIONAL MYSTERY writing as VL Kazarian

(Detectives Ruiz, Grasso and Flores):

Swift Horses Racing – Silicon Valley Murder Book 1

Across the Red Sky – Silicon Valley Murder Book 2

A Tree of Poison – Silicon Valley Murder Book 3

About Victoria Kazarian

Victoria Kazarian lives and writes in San Jose, California. After working for years as a Silicon Valley marketing professional, she taught high school English and actually owned a bread bakery of her own called The Laughing Loaf.

When she's not writing, she enjoys baking artisan breads and forcing her children and dog to go on road trips to the Pacific Northwest. See what she's up to at victoriakazarian.com

You can contact Victoria—or perhaps leave a message for Gracie Markley herself—at TheLaughingLoaf@gmail.com

Laughing Loaf Bakery Recipes

Old Fashioned Gingerbread Cookies
Dark Matter Gingerbread
Triple Gingersnaps

Old Fashioned Gingerbread Cookies

Soft, chewy gingerbread cookies.

You can make them regular or gluten free. Half my family is gluten intolerant and they love the flavor—these cookies do not taste "less than" as gluten free cookies.

    1/3 cup softened shortening—Or you can use butter or even margarine (don't use light or low fat, though)

    1 cup brown sugar

    1-1/2 cups dark molasses

    1/2 cup very cold water

    5 to 5-1/2 cups all-purpose flour (To make these gluten free, use King Arthur Gluten Free flour or Bob's Red Mill Cup-for-Cup)

    1 teaspoon salt

    1 teaspoon allspice

    1 teaspoon cloves

    1-1/2 teaspoon cinnamon

    1-1/2 teaspoon ginger

Mix these two ingredients in a small bowl or glass:

2 teaspoons baking soda
3 tablespoons cold water.

Mix first three ingredients. Then add the 1/2 cup of cold water. Now sift the flour, salt, and spices into the wet mixture then pour in your water and baking soda mixture. Mix dough till well blended.

Chill the dough in the fridge for at least 30 minutes.

Then preheat the oven to 350 degrees.

Sprinkle flour lightly on a clean, flat surface. Roll the dough out to 1/2-inch thickness with a rolling pin.

Use cookie cutters or even the rim of a glass, floured lightly, to cut out your cookies.

Bake for 15-17 minutes. The cookies will puff up as they bake, then may slowly go down after you take them out. They will smell amazing.

Let them cool for 15 minutes before eating or frosting them.

Triple Gingersnaps

For true ginger lovers.

3/4 cup butter
1 cup sugar, plus a bowl of sugar to roll the dough balls in
1 egg
1/4 cup molasses
2 cups flour
2 teaspoons baking soda
1/2 teaspoon salt
1 teaspoon cinnamon
2 teaspoons powdered ginger
2 teaspoons grated ginger root
3/4 cup of finely cut-up crystallized ginger pieces (I use Trader Joe's)

Preheat oven to 350 degrees; grease cookie sheets. Beat together softened butter and the 1 cup of sugar. Add egg then beat till fluffy, then add molasses. Stir together the flour, baking soda, salt, cinnamon, and gingers, then add to wet ingredients. Stir till well blended. Form dough into 1-inch balls and then roll them in the sugar. Bake for about 10- 11 minutes, until they puff up and are light brown. Cool on a rack. Makes about three dozen.

Dark Matter Gingerbread Cake

Rich and warming; works well with regular all-purpose flour or gluten-free flour.

Preheat oven to 325 degrees.

Mix these dry ingredients thoroughly in a medium-sized bowl:

2-1/2 cups regular all-purpose flour
OR gluten-free flour (King Arthur or Bob's Red Mill Cup-for-Cup work best)
1-1/2 teaspoons baking soda
1/2 teaspoon baking powder
3 teaspoons ground cinnamon
2 teaspoons ground ginger
1/2 teaspoon allspice
1/4 teaspoon ground cloves
3/4 teaspoon sea salt
1/2 cup granulated sugar
1/2 cup packed dark brown sugar

Dark Matter Gingerbread Cake

Mix the following ingredients well in a bowl, then blend into the dry ingredients bowl:

1 cup warm water
3/4 cup molasses
1 (4 ounce) stick of softened butter
2 tablespoons olive oil
1 large egg

Mix batter until smooth. Pour into the square pan, but only till the batter comes about a 1/2" to 3/4" up the side of the pan. If you have excess, pour it into a cupcake tin—that's your personal baker's portion! Set both pans on a rack in middle of the preheated oven and set the timer for 25 minutes.

It may rise up fairly high but it will fall after you take it out and there will be a bit of a dip in the middle (that part will be the moistest and richest).

Sift powdered sugar over it, or slice and top each with a dollop of whipped cream. Serve warm.

Gingerbread and Left for Dead playlist

To sing along with the Christmas music Gracie and Beck sing as they bake, listen to the *Gingerbread & Left for Dead* playlist on Spotify.

Gingerbread & Left for Dead playlist